To Jacob and Tony Hiss
— S.M.

Go to www.scholastic.com for Web site information
on Scholastic authors and illustrators.

Library of Congress Cataloging-in-Publication Data
Metzger, Steve.
    It's beach day! / by Steve Metzger; illustrated by Hans Wilhelm.
       p.   cm. — (Dinofours)
    "Cartwheel books."
    Summary: Although at first Tara's fear of water keeps her on the beach, she thinks of all the brave things she has done and decides to join the other Dinofours in the water.
    ISBN 0-590-03267-4
    [1. Beaches — Fiction.   2. Fear — Fiction.   3. Dinosaurs — Fiction.]
   I. Wilhelm, Hans, 1945- ill. II. Title. III. Series: Metzger, Steve. Dinofours.
PZ7.M56775Dgi   1998
[E]—dc21
                                          97-43277
                                          CIP
                                          AC

10 9 8 7 6 5 4 3   9/9 0/0 01 02

Printed in the U.S.A.   24
First printing, May 1998

DINOFOURS™
IT'S BEACH DAY!

by Steve Metzger
Illustrated by Hans Wilhelm

Cartwheel
·B·O·O·K·S·®

SCHOLASTIC INC.
New York Toronto London Auckland Sydney

It was a hot June morning. Mrs. Dee gathered the children on the rug.

"What day is it today?" she asked.

"Beach Day!" everyone shouted.

"We're going to Dino Beach," Joshua called out.

"To swim in the ocean," added Danielle.

"Yes," said Mrs. Dee. "You'll be able to go in the ocean, but only up to your knees. That's where the waves won't be too high or too rough."

"Tara will be the first one in," said Albert. "She's not afraid of the waves. She's brave."

The other children nodded.

I'm not always brave, Tara thought.

"Okay," said Mrs. Dee, looking out the window. "The bus is here."

Mrs. Dee turned to the parents and baby-sitters in the classroom. "I'm so glad you could join us on our trip," she said.

Mrs. Dee reviewed the safety rules. Then, she asked the children to get their lunches and towels and line up at the door.

"I'm first," said Brendan.

"So what," said Tracy. "I'm second, and second is better than first."

"No, it isn't!"

"Yes, it is!"

"Okay," said Mrs. Dee. "Let's go. The bus driver is waiting."

The grown-ups helped the children get on the bus and buckle their seat belts. When they were settled, the driver started the engine.

"Shall we sing a song?" asked Mrs. Dee from the front seat.

Tara didn't feel like singing. She looked out the window and thought about the beach. This would be her first time in the ocean.

I'm not going in the water if I don't want to, she said to herself.

Everyone sang "The Wheels on the Bus" as the bus rolled along.
All of the children had such a good time singing...except Tara.
Finally, the bus reached Dino Beach.
Mrs. Dee stood up and turned around.
"Here's what we're going to do," she said. "First, we'll find a good place to put our towels. Then, we'll go in the water."
The children cheered...except Tara.

They all walked off the bus. Tara stared at the ocean. It was even bigger than she thought it would be. Then she sang a song:

I won't go in the water!
I won't go in at all!
The ocean is so big, big, BIG!
And I feel very small.

When they found a good spot, the parents and baby-sitters helped the children spread out their towels. Mrs. Dee put down cones to mark off their space.

"You must stay inside the cones," Mrs. Dee said to the children. "That's a very important rule. Do you understand?"

The children all said, "Yes."

"It's time to go in the water," said Mrs. Dee. "Remember, only up to your knees. Now, is there anyone who doesn't want to go in?"

Tara raised her hand.

The other Dinofours were very surprised.

"Okay, Tara," said Mrs. Dee. "Here's a pail and shovel for you to play with. Danielle's mother will stay with you."

Tara watched the children happily run into the ocean. Some jumped over the waves; others raced in and out of the water. Tara wanted to join them, but she was still afraid.

"Is everything okay, Tara?" Danielle's mother asked.

"Yes," said Tara in a low voice. "I just don't want to go in."

Tara wished she wasn't afraid of the ocean. Then, she began to think about times when she had acted bravely.

I remember climbing to the top of the climber when the other children wouldn't, she thought.

I remember holding the lizard that the pet store owner brought to school—and the other kids didn't want to touch it.

Tara began to smile.

And I remember going down the high slide by myself for the very first time.
Tara stood up.

"I am brave!" she said out loud.
Just then, Mrs. Dee walked over.

"Tara," she said, "everyone is having such a good time in the ocean. Are you sure you don't want to join them?"

"I do, Mrs. Dee!" Tara said in a strong voice.

"That's great!" Mrs. Dee said. "Do you want to hold my hand?"

"Okay," replied Tara.

Tara slowly edged toward the water. As the first wave reached her, she took a few steps back. When the next wave came, she let it wash over her feet.

It feels cold…but good, Tara thought as she dropped Mrs. Dee's hand.

With each wave, Tara went out a little farther. At one point, she stopped and thought about turning back.

I can do it, Tara told herself. She began walking again.
Finally, she was right next to Joshua.

"We're playing a great game," Joshua said to Tara. "When the
wave comes, we jump and say, 'Go away!'"

Tara joined in. Soon, she was laughing and jumping way up high.

After a while, it was time to leave the water and eat lunch. As Tara towelled herself dry, she sang a new song:

I love the beach! I love the beach!
The waves, the sand, the sun.
Can we come back tomorrow?
The beach is so much fun!